Finn
·AT CLEE POINT·

For Mum — R. K.
To Laura — G. M.

Barefoot Books
2067 Massachusetts Ave
Cambridge, MA 02140

Text copyright © 2012 by Richard Knight
Illustrations copyright © 2012 by Giovanni Manna
The moral rights of Richard Knight and Giovanni Manna have been asserted

First published in the United States of America by Barefoot Books, Inc in 2012
All rights reserved

Graphic design by Graham Webb, Design Principals, England
Cover design by Mary Ann Guillette, Cambridge, MA, USA
Reproduction by B & P International, Hong Kong
Printed in China on 100% acid-free paper
This book was typeset in Carmina, Mousse Script,
Lobster Hand and Neutra Text
The illustrations were prepared in watercolors on cotton paper

ISBN 978-1-84686-401-8

Library of Congress Cataloging-in-Publication Data
is available under LCCN 2011044735

1 3 5 7 9 8 6 4 2

Finn

·AT CLEE POINT·

Written by Richard Knight
Illustrated by Giovanni Manna

Barefoot Books
step inside a story

CONTENTS

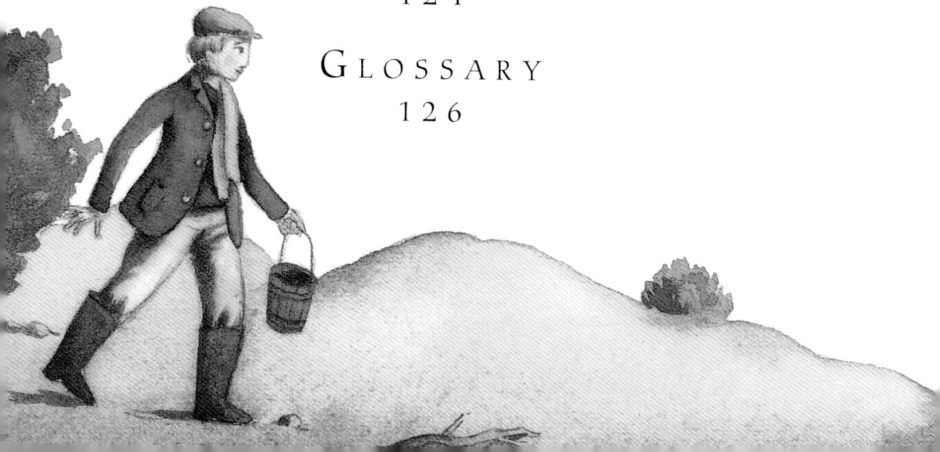

CHAPTER ONE

DOWN AT CLEE POINT

It was Dan Quigley who taught me to set lines, the day before my tenth birthday. Out at the mouth of the river the mudflats stretched endlessly toward the horizon. There, Quigley showed me how to drive the wooden stakes deep into the sand and tie the line fast to them, each hook fastened with a half-blood knot and a fat lugworm threaded on.

"Always give yourself at least an hour before the tide turns, son. Don't want to swim home, do you?" He stood, straightening his stiff back, and looked at the line stretching along the bank of the creek. "And better hope the gulls don't eat the worms before the tide covers 'em."

The tides were dangerous down there. All day and all night the sea lashed away at the land, altering its shape. Our lives in Seamer Bay depended on the sea, but we knew from an early age that it was a two-faced friend. It fed us and provided our living, but it could destroy lives too.

We returned the next morning, before sunrise, striding
out into the darkness, the thick mud sucking at our boots.
I was ten that day but felt almost like a man, following
Quigley's yellow oilskins out toward the water. Close to
the edge we heard the shrieks and then saw the circling
gulls in the faint light rising from the east.

"Yah! Yah!" Quigley ran at them, swinging an empty
bucket around and around above his head. I stood and
laughed. But when I caught up with him, standing next to
the uncovered line, my heart soared and wheeled like those
gulls. Ten silver fish I counted, flapping on the sand. "Not
bad for thirty hooks and your first line, Finn."

He grinned and pinched my cold ear. Quigley was old
and worn out, his hair as gray as a winter sky. But behind
the beard and matted hair there was a kind face and he
taught me well. He didn't fish with the other men any
more. He made his living from crab and lobster pots a mile
or two offshore.

"I'm too old to be going after herring or hauling lines
in," he laughed.

Dad wasn't so sure of Quigley.

"What's he want to hang around with a boy for?" he
said as he stood buttoning his jacket in the doorway, on his
way out to The Anchor by the harbor wall. "It's strange,

if you ask me." But it didn't feel strange to me. The wind slammed the door shut behind him.

That autumn I set lines on my own for the first time, when Quigley was busy checking his pots. Down at the edge of the tide you could hear the roar of the open sea at the mouth of the estuary. I'd been warned many times not to go to the end of the point. Clee Point was a thin finger of sand and scrub that curled out into the sea to the southeast of Seamer Bay. It was fast being worn away by winter storms. Quigley said that one day soon it would be breached by the sea, leaving an island completely cut off from the point.

"You keep away from those folk down there, Finn Greer. They're no good," Ma said.

Dad looked over his newspaper. "And if they don't get you, the river will. So keep away, you hear?"

"They" were the Finers, a family who scraped a living from the sea and the shore at the end of the point. They were rarely seen in Seamer Bay. If Mr. Finer did come, he'd spend most of the day after market in The Anchor, alone in a corner, according to Dad. The villagers had little to do with him, nor he with them.

"I don't know why he wants to live right down there, in the middle of nowhere. Perhaps he thinks we're not good enough for him," Dad snorted, turning over the page of his newspaper.

"Why's that?" I asked. Dad glanced up at Ma, who was peeling potatoes at the kitchen table. I saw her shake her head.

"Oh nothing, Finn. Water under the bridge and all that." He folded his paper and threw it on the table.

The older village children sometimes used to scare their little brothers and sisters with stories about Clee Point and Finer's graveyard.

"You keep out their way or you'll end up in Finer's graveyard with all the others," they'd say, and you could see the eyes of the little ones widen in horror. I had no brother or sister to tease like that and I'd never been down to the point, so I paid little attention to the stories. But on the few occasions when I'd seen Mr. Finer walking through the village, I'd felt the force of the stares he had to endure, and noticed the small children clinging to their mothers' skirts. I didn't know why the Finers were outcasts. I'd never asked. It was just the way things were.

We thought Mr. Finer's children, Kitty and Davey, were wild. The high tides and storms made it a treacherous journey from Clee Point, and in the middle of winter it was rare to see them at school. When they did make the long and difficult walk there, they spent break times at the far edge of the yard, talking to nobody but each other. From time to time some of the boys would try to provoke Kitty and Davey with insults and shoves, but it never worked and they would soon lose interest. I had little to do with either of them. The only thing I knew about them was that they had no mother.

"She ended up in Finer's graveyard, like all the others," one of my friends said one day, grinning.

"You don't expect me to believe that, do you? I'm not a little kid!" I laughed.

CHAPTER TWO

THE CONTEST

One day at school, early in October, we were sent into the hall where old Joe McKinnon, chairman of the Fishermen's Committee, stood at the front next to Mr. Nevin, the headmaster. We sat down in rows wondering why he was there.

As the last class entered, the hall fell silent. Joe looked small and nervous in front of us, his thick gray hair molded above his forehead from years of steering into the wind. He fiddled with the buttons on his woolen jacket and tried not to catch anybody's eye.

Mr. Nevin spoke for a long time, until our backsides ached from the hard, polished floor. He talked about the village, and the gratitude we should all show to the Fishermen's Committee.

"They help you and your families in many different ways," he said, peering out over the tops of his steel-rimmed glasses. Old Joe shuffled, and looked up at us briefly. "They ensure a good, fair price for everyone's catch. They organize rescues at sea. And they raise money to look after the families of fishermen who cannot work because of illness or injury."

We knew all this already. We had been brought up knowing these men. Dad had never been on the committee as far as I knew, but some of my friends' dads were. And Joe had been the chairman for as long as I could remember.

"It's all a fix," Dad would snort. "Funny how the boats of the committee members always seem to get the best prices at market." He didn't care much for old Joe. "He thinks he owns Seamer Bay, that one. Time someone younger had a go, if you ask me."

We began to shuffle, but Mr. Nevin hadn't quite finished.

"You all know Mr. McKinnon of the Fishermen's Committee. He would like to make a special announcement. So sit up straight and listen carefully."

Old Joe cleared his throat and tried to smile. It seemed out of place. The only time he ever spoke to us was to pass a message to our dads or to tell us off for hanging around the fish market, getting in the way.

"Here in our little village it is the sea which provides your fathers and mothers with their living. It's a difficult life, dangerous sometimes. Fifty years ago this December, the first Fishermen's Committee was elected to try and help the village work together to make everyone's lives easier. And as a way of celebrating, the committee would like me to make a special announcement. Put your hand up if you have ever set a line on the shore?" Glancing around at each other, about ten or twelve of us put our hands cautiously in the air. Joe McKinnon nodded slowly. "Good…good. Well, I have news for you! The Fishermen's Committee has decided that there is to be an annual fishing contest, beginning this year, to celebrate its fiftieth anniversary."

There was an excited murmur from the children around me. Old Joe waited until it had died down before continuing.

"On the first Saturday of December, children under the age of twelve can set a line of one hundred hooks at low tide." There was a groan from the top two classes behind us. The headmaster raised his hand and the noise quickly died down. Joe continued: "You should collect your catch on the Sunday morning, and bring it to the fish market after church. The one with the most fish will win this…"

We watched with curiosity as he turned and put his hand into a cloth bag on the floor and pulled out a model boat. I recognized it instantly. It had sat, for as long as any of us could remember, in the window of The Anchor down

by the harbor. We passed by there most days, and even now we still stopped to wonder at the boat. It was carved from wood, painted blue and white. There was so much detail; the rigging for the sails, little kits, boxes, ropes and tiny model people on the deck. It sat on a polished wooden stand where a brass plate had been fixed. As old Joe held it up for us to see there were gasps around the room.

"So, one of you will be the very first to have your name on the plate here and will get to keep the boat for a year. Remember, the first Saturday in December. Are there any questions?" He placed the boat carefully back in the bag. There was a long pause as he looked around the room, until finally his gaze came to rest directly on me. "Yes?" he asked. I was silent, struck dumb. Why was he looking at me? My hands had remained in my lap. I had nothing to ask him.

Suddenly there came a calm voice from just behind me.

"What if somebody cheats?"

Instantly a dark shadow seemed to pass across old Joe McKinnon's face.

"Cheat? How could anybody cheat?" He glanced at the headmaster, who was busy watching the speaker. The owner of the voice had no fear of the men in front of us. It rose again, bright and clear behind me.

"Well, they could set two hundred hooks. They could set two lines. They could set a line on Friday night as well and keep the fish iced."

Joe's face reddened a little. It was clear he had not thought of this. He stared for a moment, until suddenly an answer seemed to strike him.

"An adult must go with you to collect the line, to check. Ask your fathers." Joe stared at the person behind me for a moment. Even though I knew he wasn't looking at me now, I felt uncomfortable and shifted a little to one side. "But I'm sure nobody here would want to bring shame on their family like that," he said and, briefly nodding at Mr. Nevin, left the hall without another word.

Later, as we all filed out, I looked across to see who had spoken. It was a small, pale-faced boy with dark hair, a mischievous smile slung across his lips. It was Davey Finer.

In the yard that afternoon we boasted and talked up our chances in the contest with each other. Despite the laughter in the air as we left to go home, there was little doubt that this was to be a serious business. Each of us desperately wanted to win. Leaving school by the other gate, alone, was Davey Finer. But I think only I noticed him go.

CHAPTER THREE

AT THE EDGE OF THE TIDE

Quigley sat on an upturned basket and helped me tie hooks on the line. We coiled it carefully into a large metal bucket, laying sheets of newspaper between each hook.

"Quigley?" I stopped coiling the line for a second.

"Yes, son?" he replied, his head still bowed to the task.

"Why don't people like the Finers much?"

Quigley stopped and looked up at me. He laid the line on the rim of the bucket and stood up, arching his stiff back.

"Well. There's a question. Not sure I have an answer for it though," he said.

"Dad says he thinks he's too good for us. That's why he keeps away, down the point. And his kids, they don't fit in at school either. Nobody likes 'em much."

"And you, Finn? Do you like 'em?" Quigley sat back down on his basket.

The truth was, I didn't know whether I liked them. "I've never talked to them much," I said.

Quigley nodded slowly. "Well. Bill Finer, he's a little… different, shall we say?"

"What do you mean?" I asked.

"Well, he don't go to church for a start." Quigley looked at me and smiled.

"Neither do you, Quigley!"

He laughed. "True enough." He thought for a moment. "Well, he don't pay much mind to the committee. Maybe that's it. He's not Joe McKinnon's best friend, that's for sure."

"Have they ever lived in the village?" I asked.

Quigley sat down on the basket again. "All these questions!" He paused, watching me closely. "Yes, but it was before you were born, Finn. He used to work on the boats, before…" he hesitated, and I sensed something difficult, something he wasn't sure he should say.

Suddenly the back door opened and Dad came down the steps with a cup of steaming tea in his hand.

"Hey, Quigley, don't you have anything better to do?"

Quigley looked up for a moment, then across at me as I tied another half-blood knot to fix the line to the end stake. He'd taught me to do that. Quigley looked back at Dad, and seemed a little puzzled.

22

"No, Tom. Not that I can think of. You want to help us?" He held out a hook and some twine. "We need all the help we can get. Right, Finn?"

I looked up at Dad and grinned hopefully. He took a mouthful of tea then brushed his lips on his sleeve.

"Nah. Hey, and Finn? Don't you go too far down Clee Point, remember?"

He turned quickly around and headed back through the open door into the kitchen.

On Saturday morning I took my bike and a small line down the road to the point. It was a bright, clear day and the ribbed mudflats shimmered under the low-angled autumn sunlight. Leaving my bike by the side of the single-track road among the buckthorn bushes laden with orange berries, I walked out in the direction of a creek on the estuary side, where I'd set lines before.

Walking across the mud, I began to think. Everyone knew the best fish were out at the mouth of the river. If I were to win, maybe it would be worth the risk? It was a clear day —what harm could I come to? And anyway, there wasn't a soul around for miles. Ma and Dad would never know. So I carried on past the creek and followed the edge of the tide down Clee Point, which bent southwards into the sea. Curlews shrieked wildly above my head, warning me back.

After walking for ten minutes I found another creek, deeper and wider than the first, where the river water was already beginning to flow. I'd never been this far down the point before. It felt wild and open and dangerous, but exciting too. The breeze had stiffened now and was beginning to gust a little. Beyond the river, I noticed some thick clouds boiling up from the southwest and starting to cross the water in my direction, covering the blue sky and sun. With the tide flooding fast and the weather closing in, I knew I'd have to be quick.

I set the line along the edge of the creek, like Quigley had shown me. The tips of my fingers began to feel numb in the wind, as they worked hurriedly to hook the worms on. The sand was a little firmer and more ribbed here, and I had to stand on top of the stakes to sink them in. But eventually everything was set and I stood looking out across the river, waiting for the incoming tide to cover the line.

I gazed at the emptiness of the world around me and all at once felt completely alone, with only the wind, the birds and the low rushing of the river for company. There was

a sudden updraft of wind, and soon afterward the first drops of rain began to slant into my face. I shivered under my coat and turned quickly for the road, leaving the line to be covered.

For a brief moment I was confused by the large expanse of water racing between me and the road. But when I turned back to face the river, the confusion was replaced by a sudden jolt of fear. I was trapped. On three sides the river water had surrounded me. Only further south, even further out, along Clee Point, was there a stretch of beach. I ran along it as fast as I could, the bucket bobbing frantically in my hand, buffeted by the wind. I remember thinking then that even if I did beat the tide, Dad and Ma would surely find out I had disobeyed them.

And that would mean the end of the contest for me.

CHAPTER FOUR

A HELPING HAND

As I ran I could sense the water racing in all around me, but I didn't dare look. My eyes, watering in the wind, were focused intently on the end of the point where the stretch of beach would lead me, if I ever made it that far. It was after a few minutes running next to the water's edge that I became aware of something moving toward me. I glanced to the right and there, heading toward me from the middle of the river, was a small, white coble with a red mainsail. A figure, too far away for me to recognize, leaned out to one side and shouted, waving its arms frantically. But the voice was lost on the wind. I stopped and strained my ears against the rushing river.

"Stay there!" The boat drew right into the shore, tacking back and forth, and I saw that the figure was only a boy, about my own age. Then he beckoned wildly to me. "Come on! Quick!"

I realized I was supposed to wade through the water to the boat. The first time the water came over the top of my boots, my whole body shook with cold. As I got nearer, I lifted my head and saw a face through the rain, a face I knew. It was Davey Finer.

"Get in! Come on, give me your hand!" He leaned over the gunwales of the boat as I threw the bucket aboard and grasped his outstretched hands. They felt warm after the cold of the water. It hurt my stomach as he hauled me in like a net of fish over onto the slimy deck. He sat down on a bench by the small cuddy and smiled, that same mischievous smile I had seen in the school hall.

"Not the right weather for paddling really, is it?" Then he quickly moved past me into the stern and grasped the tiller, swinging the boat back in toward the middle of the river.

"Mind your head!" he shouted just in time before the boom of the mainsail swung past above me.

I sat in the bow near the cuddy. The bow spray hit me full in the face as the boat bounced and strained through choppy water where the sea and the river clashed. The wooden deck was covered in a tangle of black line tied with hooks. I noticed a kit half full of cod and whiting. The glassy eyes stared lifelessly back at me. Some of the hooks on the line still had fish on them. Davey must have been long-lining from the boat and in the middle of unhooking the fish when he spotted me.

"You can take the rest of them off if you want something to do." I looked up and saw him watching me. He said very little else to me until we had moored the boat. Davey had sailed to a jetty near a small wooden house at the very end of Clee Point. By the time we had reached it and he had used a long boat hook to pull us right in, a storm was building.

We stood outside the door to the house.

"You were lucky there. Them tides are so fast they can cut you off in a couple of minutes. We'll go in now. Take us as you find us." He smiled at my hesitation. "I know what they say about Dad in the village. But he's not as bad as you've been told." I nodded and followed him through the large black door.

Inside it was warm and still. We stood in the kitchen, my trousers dripping seawater onto the stone floor.

"Dad!" Davey shouted through the house. After a few seconds there was the creak of a door opening at the far end of the kitchen and Mr. Finer appeared suddenly, a dark and brooding presence that filled the room. He was a tall man with black hair, an unshaven face and slightly stooping shoulders. He looked me up and down slowly. I was not

sure whether to speak first. My jaws and teeth began to tremble with cold.

"Well, well. Hello there, young 'un."

He looked at Davey, who shrugged his shoulders.

"Picked Finn up off Fleet Sand. Tide was trapping him."

Mr. Finer continued to look, his face solemn, but not severe. He sat down at a large old table in the middle of the kitchen and stared at the puddle that had collected around my feet, drumming his fingers on the wood.

"Well, are you going to go and find some dry clothes for our guest, Davey?"

CHAPTER FIVE

THE FINERS

Kitty Finer was a year older, in the class above me at school, and when she came into the kitchen she smiled. If she was surprised to find me there, she didn't show it. I looked away quickly. It was a warm smile, but she looked at me so calmly and confidently that I suddenly felt very young next to her. I couldn't meet her eyes. Without even saying a word she'd managed to make me feel ashamed. I'd never hurt her, or Davey, but I'd never spoken to them either. I'd joined the other children in the silence of the village.

"Here, Finn. Go in there and get out of those wet things before you catch a chill," Mr. Finer said, handing me a bundle of clothes that Davey had brought in and pointing to the kitchen door. I felt my face redden as Kitty watched me squelching uncomfortably across the stone floor. In the dark room behind the door was a tattered old sofa and armchair. A small table in the middle of the room had a starched white cloth under a vase of sea holly. I didn't know why, but it wasn't the kind of thing I'd expected to see. Using the towel Davey had brought with the clothes, I dried myself quickly and put the clothes and socks on. Davey was a little smaller than me and the trousers wouldn't quite button at the top.

"Give 'em to Kitty. She'll dry 'em for you, won't you, Kit?" Mr. Finer said, looking at the wet clothes I held under one arm while trying to keep the trousers up with my other hand. Kitty walked slowly over toward me and held out her arms. I smiled timidly and let the bundle fall into them. She pulled a wooden clotheshorse from a corner and set the clothes to dry in front of the fire at the far end of the room.

"Those a bit tight there, Finn?" Mr. Finer smiled, looking at my hand clutching the tops of the trousers. He glanced at Kitty, but she was busy with my clothes. It didn't feel right, her doing that for me. I'd never even said hello to her before. "Davey's a bit of a skinny rake, aren't you, son?" Davey glowered at his dad, who laughed warmly at him across the other side of the table. "But strong, though! Very strong. Here, watch!" Mr. Finer twisted around and placed his elbow on the table. I looked on as Davey grasped his dad's open hand and they began to arm wrestle. They went backward and forward, Davey straining and his father barely breaking sweat. Suddenly I noticed a faint grin on Mr. Finer's face and a second or two later he let his own arm be forced flat to the table. "Got me again!" I laughed out loud. Kitty stood by the clotheshorse, shaking her head.

We all drank tea and talked for a while. Mr. Finer was nothing like the person I'd imagined him to be.

"Can you play chess, Finn? It's a grand game. Isn't that right, Kitty?" Kitty was sitting at the end of the table, reading. She flashed another smile at us over the top of her book, but said nothing. He brought a wooden chess set from the sideboard and Davey helped him lay out the carved pieces.

"I'll play you, and Finn can help me," Davey said to his dad, when the board was set up. "He'll learn the moves that way."

I spent the rest of the afternoon with them at the table as my clothes dried in front of the fire, trying to remember all the different moves. Davey was quiet and I noticed how his father often tried to draw him into the conversation. When Davey did talk, though, he was funny and warm. If I forgot the way the knights moved, he would patiently show me again.

As the sky began to darken outside, it struck me how little I knew Davey. We'd hardly spoken ten words in several years at school. Yet here I was, eating, drinking and laughing with him and his family while outside the storm rattled the wooden boards of the house, threatening to carry it off to sea. Everyone said to keep away from them, but I felt so welcome there in that kitchen. And it didn't seem to make any sense.

"So Finn, how do you like your friends at school?" Kitty asked, putting her book down.

I looked through the window behind her, where you could just catch sight of waves crashing onto the beach. "They're all right, I suppose…" I wasn't sure what to say.

"That's good. Good that you have friends." With that she glanced at Davey, then smiled and picked her book up again. Mr. Finer looked at his daughter and laughed.

"She's a proper bookworm. I suppose living here she has to be, eh? Two men and no company for three miles!" He winked at me.

As darkness fell, I put on my steaming clothes. They weren't quite dry, and they smelled strongly of seawater, but I hoped Ma wouldn't notice if she was busy with supper.

"Bye, Finn." Kitty looked up from her book as I left.

"Bye." I couldn't bring myself to use her name.

Mr. Finer and Davey walked me back along the single-track road, to where I'd left my bicycle in the buckthorn bushes.

"What about your line?" Davey asked. I'd completely forgotten about it in all the excitement of the day.

"Well, I was going to leave it for a double tide, overnight. I'll get up early tomorrow and pick it up."

Davey and his father exchanged a knowing glance.

"Davey'll meet you here at seven and help you out. If that's all right with you, Finn?" What could I say? Mr. Finer held out his hand, which felt rough and warm as I shook it.

"OK. See you at seven, Davey." I imagined Dad and Ma still in bed, as I secretly crept out of the house.

We said good-bye and I pedaled hard down the road, reaching home just before dark.

"Where've you been?" Ma wiped her hands on her apron. Three codling lay on a wooden board on the table, waiting for her to wash them. The smell of the sea wafted in as I closed the kitchen door behind me. I hoped she wouldn't notice my damp clothes. From the table, the dark eyes of the fish seemed to stare back at me accusingly.

"Oh, just down by the river setting a line," I called, already climbing the stairs two at a time.

My answer wasn't a lie, but it held one somewhere within it.

39

Davey was already there as I cycled up in the darkness to the spot where we'd parted the evening before. There were still tiny scratches of stars in the inky sky to the west. To the east, across the sea, was a faint yellow line on the horizon. It was going to be a clear morning. Davey smiled at me and pointed at my bucket.

"You sure that's going to be big enough?"

I grinned, and we began to trudge out toward the low-water mark. He didn't speak much and it was hard to think of things to say. The boys at school kept him out of everything but I didn't understand why. Maybe his shyness had something to do with it? And I'd been just as cold to him as the other boys had, when I thought about it.

The tops of the stakes were visible in the shallow water and we stood, waiting. I became more and more excited as we watched the water gradually recede. First, I saw a couple of fish on the near end of the line, which I threw into the bucket, but soon we were both working fast to unhook them all and the bucket was full. Twenty hooks; sixteen fish.

"That's the best line I've ever set!" I could hardly contain myself, picturing my hands on the blue-and-white boat.

"Yeah. It's a good place here. But even better there." He pointed to a creek half a mile downriver. "Mind, you need to be careful around here when the tide turns."

"Are you going to set a line too?" I asked, thankful for a shared interest.

He studied my face for a second, then smiled and looked out at the river.

"Nah. We fish to eat, not to win prizes." He looked at the empty line, the unburdened twine and hooks now flapping in the wind. "But take some advice, if you like. Put it in that creek. Lay it in a zigzag, along the edge, then the last twenty hooks across to the other side. And leave the line a little lower to the ground. And Finn?" I looked up, and saw him watching the gulls shrieking above our heads, their eyes fixed on the bucket brimming with fish. "A handful of sand to cover each hook will stop the gulls and the crabs eating the worms."

CHAPTER SIX

OUTCASTS

Dad threw his newspaper on the table and rested both hands on the back of a chair.

"I thought I'd made it clear, Finn! You've disobeyed me!" He glared at me as Ma turned from the sink, drying her hands on a towel.

"What's he done?" She looked from Dad to me and back again, worried. Dad's eyes were fixed on me and I had to meet his gaze. Eventually he turned to Ma.

"I saw Bill Finer today, in The Anchor. It seems Finn has been down on Clee Point." Ma breathed in sharply and mumbled something to herself that I couldn't hear properly. I looked down again at the table, tracing the grain of the wood with my finger.

"You haven't, have you? After all we've said, Finn. How could you? Anything could have…" Ma sat down on one of the kitchen chairs.

"Ah, but that's not the whole story, Maggie! I've been told that our Finn has been in their house, no less!" I felt him turn back to look at me again. "Asking after you he was, like a long-lost friend! They're not our kind, Finn! We've told you to keep away from him. He's a dangerous man!"

I dared a glance up, and saw Ma and Dad looking at each other. Ma spoke, her voice firm but even. "Go to your room, Finn. Your father and I need to talk about this."

I stopped in the doorway, speaking for the first time even though the words stuck in my throat. "Did he tell you why I was there?" There was a trace of anger in my voice which I'd failed to mask. Dad turned quickly, and I knew from his face I'd made a mistake.

"GO!" he shouted. I climbed the stairs two at a time.

Through the floorboards of my room I could hear the muffled sound of talking. A sense of dread welled inside me. I'd talked about nothing else but the contest for days and if they were searching for a punishment… I tried not to listen too hard. Why were the Finers such outcasts? To me there didn't seem much you could dislike about them, but Dad's opinion on them was as clear as the Pole Star in the night sky.

Dad came into my room and sat on the bed next to me. I could hear Ma clearing dishes in the kitchen downstairs.

He seemed a little calmer now, taking a long breath before beginning to speak.

"I don't suppose you can imagine how shameful it is to have a man tell you he helped your son, and me not even knowing you'd been in danger?"

He waited, but I couldn't think how to answer. Nothing I thought of sounded much like the right reply, the kind of thing an adult might say. He stood stiffly and walked to the window.

"You like setting lines, then?" He spoke to the view through the glass.

"I suppose."

"And you thought Clee Point would be a good place to fish?" He turned around and I nodded briefly, before looking away. "Yeah. And a good place to drown too, Finn." His voice was soft, almost sad.

"It wasn't him," I muttered.

"What?"

"It wasn't him that rescued me. It was Davey. Mr. Finer just got me dry and fetched me home."

Dad looked thoughtful. "Who's Davey?" he asked.

"His son."

"Then I've some thanks to give Davey. I think I may have been ungrateful to his dad today." There was a brief silence before he spoke again. "I know you're growing up, Finn, but you be straight wi' me from now on. If you're going somewhere, you tell me. Right?"

He smiled, something I hadn't expected.

"Right," I mumbled.

Dad sat back down on the bed, placing his hand awkwardly on mine.

"Dad? Why does everyone treat them so badly?" I asked, looking down at the rough skin of his fingers.

Dad paused, then lifted his hand. "Just something that happened a long time ago. You wouldn't understand, Finn. Just keep away from there."

I could still feel where his hand had been, a long time after he'd gone down the stairs and out of the house.

The next day I saw Davey at break time in the yard. He was sitting on a wall with Kitty at the far edge, away from the crowds.

"Are you getting lots of practice with your line, Finn?" he said, smiling shyly.

FINN AT CLEE POINT

"Aye. You sure you won't try yourself?" I asked. "I bet you'd win."

Kitty looked up at me, her eyes squinting in the sunlight, and laughed.

"He don't need no prize to prove he can catch a fish or two! He knows more'n that lot'll ever know." She jerked her thumb toward the game of bad-tempered football being played in the yard. Some of my friends had already noticed us and had become curious, slowly wandering over. They looked Davey coolly up and down.

"Davey Finer, what's the matter? No muck on the beach to collect today?" one of them sneered. They looked at each other with cruel, mocking grins. But Davey ignored them, gazing placidly ahead, a faint smile on his lips.

For the first time I saw how we appeared in Davey's eyes and I felt ashamed. I could sense Kitty watching me, waiting for me to say something. But I said nothing. She stood up abruptly. For a moment she looked as though she was going to speak to me, but then she turned and began to walk away as my friends made faces behind her back. Davey smiled briefly at me and followed her, a few paces behind.

"What you talking to them Finers about?"

"Yeah, stick with your own kind, Finn."

"You don't like 'em, do you?" they asked when Kitty and Davey had gone.

"Nah! Come on, let's go!" I ran back across the yard to the football match.

Why hadn't Davey said anything? And Kitty, she was so strong and confident but she just ignored them all, never said a word.

On the way home later that afternoon, I saw Kitty ahead of me walking along the seawall toward the road to the point. I looked behind me. None of my friends were around.

"Hey, Kitty!" I ran up behind her, but she didn't turn. "Where's Davey?"

She stopped and smiled as I drew level. It was that same searching look, a smile that asked questions.

"Why?"

I hesitated. She must hate me, I thought. I tried to think of a reason.

"Just thought we could…" I stuttered under her gaze. She was magnificent. Her long black hair flapped wildly in the wind. I couldn't speak as I watched its jerking dance around her flushed cheeks. But she didn't seem to mind it. Then suddenly, without warning, she caught hold of her hair and clenched it in a tight fist behind her head. Her eyes softened a little.

"He went on ahead." Kitty started to walk away, turning as she went. "You know, you're all right really, Finn. You just need to be a little more sure of yourself."

Later that night, with the wind banging the shutters outside my bedroom window, those words swirled around in my head.

CHAPTER SEVEN

SECRET FRIENDS

I set several more lines during October and on into November, often in the creek that Davey had shown me. Every line produced plenty of fish; usually codling, but conger eels, dabs, flounder and whiting too. And I began to make a habit of cycling down to the end of Clee Point afterward and calling on Davey and Kitty. Sometimes we walked around the end of the spit where the sand drifted into the sea. It was so thin and flat it felt like you could walk straight out onto the waves.

Kitty knew the names of all the birds and I soon began to recognize the easier ones—oystercatchers, snipe and redshank —by their calls. I'd never really noticed how beautiful they were before. Out to sea, we could spot the boats coming back from the fishing grounds, the gulls chasing them all the way home. Sometimes I'd pick out Dad's boat by its sail, through the little telescope Davey carried with him.

When the weather was bad we'd sit in the kitchen and play chess, or just talk. I knew most of the moves now. Mr. Finer was often out, setting his own lines or on his boat, but when he came in there was always a warm smile.

"Hey there, Finn. Good to see you!" He would hang his coat behind the door and stand with his back to the fire. "So. Who's winning?"

It was always Kitty, never me or Davey. She was always several moves ahead of me. I could never see the checkmate coming.

"He's coming on, though. I reckon he could beat you!" she said to her father.

He grinned and slapped his hands together. "Right. Set 'em up and let's see, shall we?!"

On the way back home I always felt guilty, imagining the look on Ma and Dad's faces if they found out where I'd been. Yet as the weeks passed, and I came to know the family better, I discovered no good reason to think that they were right to feel that way.

One day, I found myself alone in their kitchen for a few minutes while Kitty and Davey did a job for Mr. Finer outside. My eye was caught by a faded, yellowing photograph, propped against an old lamp on the sideboard. Mr. Finer had made that sideboard himself out of driftwood.

The photograph showed a young woman, smiling at the camera. She held a baby in her arms and a little girl of about two clung to her skirt.

"That's Ma." Kitty had come in without me hearing. "It's the last photograph. She died when Davey was only a baby."

I didn't know what to say.

"I don't remember much about her." Kitty picked up the photograph. "Dad says she was the loveliest person in the world, though."

"She looks like it," I tried, but it sounded stupid.

Kitty smiled and put the photograph back against the lamp. "Yeah. She does."

"How did she die?" I asked.

"We don't know. She collapsed suddenly. Dad says he found her early one morning in the kitchen, but Dr. Ackland couldn't say why she died." She paused for a moment, gazing at the photograph. Then, as if waking suddenly from a daydream, she turned to me. "Come on."

Kitty took my hand. Her skin was soft and cool, and I felt completely in her power. She led me around the back of the house, past an outbuilding. There, in the middle of a small patch of scrubby grass, was a beautifully carved headstone. There were some white flowers tied to it, fluttering in the wind.

Finer's graveyard! So that's where the story came from.

"That's her. Dad wanted her to be buried here, instead of the churchyard in the village," Kitty said.

"Why?"

Kitty shrugged. "Don't know. They don't like us much at Seamer Bay. I think he just wanted to keep her close to us. He doesn't like to talk about it."

One afternoon the following week, I went home from school with Davey along the road. I'd told Ma I was with friends and would be back before dark, which gave me a couple of hours. It wasn't a lie. Not a real one. Dad was out on the boat and wouldn't be home until morning.

The marram grass next to the road swayed in the breeze coming off the sea to the east. That road was like a tightrope, heading out toward the end of the earth between vast expanses of water. There was something thrilling about the point, where sea and sand and sky all met. It felt like the end of everything. Or the beginning, depending on which way you faced.

We'd only walked a few hundred yards when three of my friends stepped out from behind an upturned boat at the side of the road.

"Hey, Finn!"

I nodded. "Hey."

They looked at each other and grinned.

"What you doing?" one of them asked.

My heart began to race. I shouldn't have felt so nervous. It was like I was breaking the unwritten village law: don't talk to the Finers.

"Just going home with Davey. You want to come?"

We carried on walking slowly. Now that I'd said it, I felt better. There was nothing left to hide. It felt like I'd just taken a huge step out alone into the world, leaving the village behind me on the road to Clee Point.

"Nah! What would we want to hang around with Finers for?" said another of the boys. "Come on, Finn. Let's go."

I turned and faced them. They stood in a row across the road, the sun sinking fast behind them.

"See you later, then," I said. We walked away, the wind whipping thin, twisting rivers of sand across the road in front of us.

At the house, a little later, Kitty almost fell into the kitchen, leaving the door swinging free in the wind. Mr. Finer jumped up immediately.

"Kitty! What is it?" He pushed the door shut and sat her at the table. She was crying. It felt strange seeing her like that.

"Dad, she hit me!"

Mr. Finer's face darkened, as though a cloud was passing over it. He sat next to her and spoke calmly. "Who? Who hit you?"

Kitty spluttered through her tears. "Promise you won't cause trouble, Dad!"

"Who, Kitty? Tell me." Still his voice was even.

She wiped her eyes on a handkerchief that he held out to her. I looked across at Davey, who was on the other side of the table.

"It was Mary McKinnon," he said, suddenly.

"What?" Mr. Finer's eyes widened. Mary was old Joe's granddaughter, in Kitty's class.

"She was pushing *me* around," Davey continued. I noticed a red mark on Kitty's cheek. She sniffed loudly as Davey told the story. "She said we're dirty and all kinds of other stuff. Kitty tried to stop her."

"She was waiting for me by the seawall with all her friends," Kitty took up the story.

"Why?" Mr. Finer's voice trembled a little with anger, although I could see he was trying his best to stay calm. He stroked Kitty's hair.

"Because…" she sniffed. "Dad, I'm sorry. She started it. I didn't mean to shame you…but she was saying things about Ma and…" Kitty began to cry again and Mr. Finer held her in his arms.

"You could never shame us, never. Your ma would be proud of you. You've nothing to be sorry for, Kitty. I'll speak to her granddad."

Kitty broke free and looked at him, suddenly wild-eyed. "No, Dad! Promise me! I don't want you to get in any more trouble in the village."

Mr. Finer looked worried. There was something I didn't know about, something Quigley had nearly said that time in the back garden. And if I knew what it was, I'd know why the Finers were treated like this.

CHAPTER EIGHT

JOE'S VISIT

The next day, as I was walking back from the market, just where the main street drops down to the harbor, I saw Mr. Finer standing outside The Anchor talking to old Joe McKinnon.

It was unusual to see Mr. Finer in the village at all, but I was even more surprised to see the two of them together. I stood in the shadow of a wall and watched. At first, Mr. Finer seemed to be talking softly while Joe listened. But then Mr. Finer turned to walk away and I saw Joe McKinnon say something to his back which made him spin around suddenly.

There was a dark rage in his eyes. If I hadn't seen and experienced his kindness those past few weeks, I would have been afraid.

And I could see that Joe McKinnon was afraid. I heard Mr. Finer above the wind, shouting.

"You touch even one hair on her head and I won't be responsible for my actions! You leave her be! You may be able to frighten her—she's just a girl—but not me!"

Joe was stunned, and said nothing in the face of the storm. After a moment Mr. Finer turned and marched back down the street in my direction, scowling at the ground. As he approached, I jumped up to sit on the wall and tried to look casual. Just as he was about to pass me, he looked up and stopped suddenly. For a second or two he seemed to stare right through me, but then he shook his head vigorously and smiled.

"Finn! Going anywhere special?"

I shook my head and jumped down from the wall.

"Come on. Let's go and find Davey, shall we?" He put his arm around me and made as if to carry on down the street. But then he stopped, sensing my reluctance. I was looking back at Joe McKinnon, who still stood outside The Anchor, watching us closely.

"Ah. I see. Probably best not, eh?" He didn't seem angry. I turned back and looked up at him. There was a deep sadness in his smile.

"Come on. Let's go," I said, walking on beside him. But I could feel Joe McKinnon's eyes burning into my back. It wouldn't be long before Ma and Dad had a visitor.

Sure enough, when I got home later that afternoon Joe McKinnon was sitting in a chair in the front room, the room we only ever used for guests. I'd heard his voice from outside the window.

"Finn! Is that you?" Ma called through the half-open door. "Come on in here, now." My heart thumped as I sat opposite him, on the sofa next to Ma. Dad was at sea.

"Joe's come because he's worried about you, Finn." She looked at old Joe, expecting him to continue the explanation. But he just watched me. I tried to tell myself not to be frightened. Why should I be worried about him?

But I was.

Ma waited, but soon she couldn't bear the silence. "Joe?" she said.

He glanced at her as though he'd been distracted. "I'm sorry. Finn, your mother and I have been talking about the friends you keep. We are both worried you may be mixing with the wrong sort, the sort that could lead a young lad astray." He locked the fingers of both hands together and rested them in his lap. Ma was looking from me to him and back again.

"You mean Davey and Kitty?" I asked, trying to sound brave. Joe nodded silently.

"And their father in particular," he added. I said nothing.

It was best to give nothing away. "He is a dangerous man, Finn. We want you to put an end to this friendship before you come to any harm."

My face reddened and I felt the heat rising in my head. "What harm? I'm in no danger. They're good people. Friendly. And kind, too."

Joe McKinnon smiled insincerely. "I'm sure you've heard the rumors, Finn. About Mrs. Finer?"

I nodded.

"Well, did you know she's buried down there?" I tried to look surprised, to keep my face from giving me away. I didn't want Ma to find out I'd been down on Clee Point with them. "No. And many people believe he…How can I put this?" He turned to Ma as he searched for the right words. "That he was responsible for her death, in one way or another."

I wanted to stand up and scream at him. What did he know? It was all lies, all of it. He sat there, waiting, locking and unlocking his fingers. It was like he enjoyed holding people in silence, waiting for them to make mistakes, like a spider at the edge of its web. It took all my strength, but I said nothing.

Ma followed Joe McKinnon out onto the street as he prepared to leave.

"Say thank you, Finn," she said, holding my shoulders and smiling.

"Thanks, Mr. McKinnon," I mumbled.

Joe McKinnon put a cold hand on my head for a moment, and let it drop to his side. "We only want what's best for you, Finn. Looking forward to the contest?"

I nodded. It was already the last Saturday in November and there was just one week left.

"Good, good. See you both at church next Sunday, then." And he walked slowly away down the street.

"Now, you just do as he says, and stay away from them Finers! Do you hear me, Finn?" Ma said, pulling my head round, forcing me to meet her eye. "And just hope your dad doesn't find out what you've been up to." She ushered me back inside and closed the door.

CHAPTER NINE

QUIGLEY'S STORY

The following week at school the excitement among the children reached its crisis point when two boys were sent to the headmaster for fighting in the yard. Their dispute was over fishing grounds, each claiming the right to set their line on the same stretch of beach. Other arguments raged all afternoon. I kept my distance.

The weekend before the competition, Quigley suggested we have a practice with the hundred-hook line.

"So where are you going to set it? It has to be your decision." Quigley waited, rubbing his white beard while I thought. In truth, though, I was not really thinking about where to set the line. I already knew that. But I couldn't tell anyone, not even him.

We set the line a mile upriver from Fleet Sand.

"What's this, then?" Quigley raised an eyebrow as he watched me set the line in a zigzag shape.

"Just trying something out." He nodded thoughtfully, although when I put sand over the worms and their hooks, he began to shake his head doubtfully.

"You've left it a bit late to be trying all this new stuff."

But his face was not so serious the next morning when we pulled in sixty fish, and he had to go home for a wheelbarrow and a kit to take the fish to market.

Dad was in the back garden when I came in with Quigley. He looked up briefly before turning to go inside.

"Dad! Look how much we caught today!" He turned back and I waved the money at him and smiled. I could see him thinking. Finally, a faint trace of a grin appeared on his lips.

"You go careful down there, Finn. Don't go too near Clee Point again, you hear?"

"I won't." I had to tear the lie from my lips. I was letting Dad down, I knew, but I was so desperate to win. His body was still half turned toward the back door. I looked across at Quigley, who was watching Dad.

"Finn needs an adult to go down on Sunday morning with him to pick the line up, Tom," he said. My heart jolted. I hadn't expected Quigley to say anything. If Dad agreed, I'd have to set the line somewhere else and then I wouldn't stand a chance of winning. But part of me wanted him to come, to show him what I could do on my own.

"What time?" Dad asked, finally.

"Low tide's seven, I think," I said, trying to sound as though it didn't matter.

"Don't think I'll be back in time. We're due to land about six, but maybe I could…" he began.

"Nah, doesn't matter." I fought with the muscles in my face to look relaxed. "Will you come, Quigley?"

Quigley nodded slowly, still looking at Dad.

"Sorry, Finn. I would have, but I have to earn a living, don't I, son?" Dad smiled at me and winked. Then he jerked his head toward Quigley. "Isn't it time he got a proper hobby?"

Quigley smiled back at Dad. "Well, Finn's good company for an old man like me, Tom. Keeps me on my toes with his new ideas."

Dad smiled, then turned and went inside.

There was a long silence, broken only by the shrieking of the gulls by the harbor. From our kitchen, the smell of fried fish was making me hungry. Quigley sat on an old wooden box and lit his pipe. There were often long stretches of silence with Quigley, but they were never awkward. Once, I'd asked him why he liked the quietness.

"There's music in silence, Finn, like there is in everything. When you've been at sea for a while, with the waves slapping the hull all day and night, you long for a bit of silence. Hard to find, though," he'd said.

The smoke from Quigley's pipe drifted up into the late-autumn twilight. I loved the smell of wood smoke from the chimneys and dew hanging in the air on those nights, just when the sun was going down after a cold, calm day. The weather seemed to be set fair for a couple of days, and in the morning we'd be hearing the fishermen's boots striking the cobblestones on their way down to the boats. Long-lining on a calm sea was the best, Dad said. I could hear him in the kitchen now, packing his kit bag and chatting to Ma as she cooked our supper.

"Quigley?" He took the pipe from his mouth. "You said Mr. Finer used to work on the boats. But you never told me why he stopped."

Quigley turned and looked at me, then returned the pipe to his mouth and sucked several times. I was used to waiting for an answer. He looked back up the garden to the kitchen window, as though checking to see if anyone was there.

"Well. There was a shipwreck, see. Just around the time you were born, I think. Three men lost overboard in a storm. Joe McKinnon's son was one of them."

We were used to tales of accidents and drowning. A year would rarely pass without at least one wreck, or a schoolmate losing his or her father at sea. Then a week or so later the child would return to school. We'd stand in the yard, not knowing what to say at first. But we looked after each other in our village. Nobody went hungry, and the Fishermen's Committee helped the widows and children until someone was old enough to earn their living at sea.

Quigley's pipe had gone out. He took a box of matches from his jacket pocket and struck one.

"Was that Mary's dad, then?" I asked, beginning to make sense of the story.

Quigley nodded. "Mary was just a baby," he continued, when he was sure the pipe was lit. "There was only one survivor." He scratched his stubbly chin.

"Mr. Finer?" I asked.

He nodded. "He managed to hang on to part of the broken mast and was washed ashore on the beach, a mile or so down the point. Only he knows the real story. People say he jumped and left his mates behind to drown. I've even heard people say he pushed them aside to save himself. But they weren't there. How could they know? He's the only one who knows the truth...but we've never heard it from him."

"Why not?" I asked.

"He wouldn't say anything for days afterward. By the time he'd come around a bit and begun to talk to his wife, the rumors had already started." Quigley blew the air out from his puffed cheeks. There was another silence.

"Why did he go and live down on the point, though? It don't make sense," I said.

"Finn, you're still a young lad. There's lots you don't know about adults yet. They don't always wait to judge other people."

He looked at me and smiled. We'd often sat for an hour chatting, making or mending lines together. I'd often wished I could sit with Dad doing the same things, but he was always too busy or too tired.

"Don't you get like them; people who think they can judge because they dress up for church every Sunday. I went around to see him. That's right—you were born the same day, I remember now. And Mrs. Finer was pregnant too. We talked a while. I didn't ask him about the wreck and he never told me either. Then he asked me about the old house at Clee Point."

"What'd he ask you for?" I said.

"My house, Finn." My face must have betrayed my surprise because he nodded and continued. "Belonged to my uncle, years ago. Bit of a loner, he was. When he died, it passed to me. But I had no use for it. It was empty and falling apart, so I let Bill Finer have it. He spent months rebuilding it, and he's never been back on the boats since."

It was all beginning to make sense. I knew Mr. Finer would never have abandoned his mates on that boat without good reason. But Joe McKinnon and his family blamed him for surviving the shipwreck. Mr. Finer's silence had fanned the rumors, until he couldn't face living in the village any longer.

T H E   C A T C H

Saturday arrived; the day of the contest, and I got up early to dig for the worms on the mudflats. Gray clouds were already racing up the river from the sea and a stiff breeze ruffled my hair. The mud sucked at the prongs of the garden fork as I pushed it in and levered the handle down. The briny smell of the disturbed sand became more powerful as I dug deeper and began to see the first of the fat, dark lugworms trying to slide away. Finding one hundred was going to take a good hour and an aching back.

Later that day, in the hour before darkness, I took my bike and rode down Clee Point with my line in a bucket. It was lucky that Dad had gone out to sea on the high tide early in the afternoon. Low tide wasn't until seven o'clock but the bank of the creek where I'd decided to set the line would be clear by five. As I cycled I began to spin excuses in my mind in case I was seen. But the only person I saw was

Davey, down on the road near Fleet Sand. I thought later that he might have been waiting there on purpose for me and I was pleased. I liked him more and more, now that we knew each other better. And his advice could make all the difference to my chances of winning.

"So. Today's the day?" He looked into my bucket where the line was neatly coiled. "You need a hand with the line?"

I smiled and nodded, and we walked out to the creek he'd shown me.

It was dark by the time we arrived and I was pleased Davey was there with me. We worked quickly, in silence.

There was something good about the teamwork that made the silence comfortable. Davey tapped a stake into the mud and began to unravel the twine parallel to the river, which we could hear only yards away in the darkness. I went along the line and baited the hooks quickly, patting the sand down on top of the worms. Then we stood together, calmly waiting for the tide to turn, the smell of worms, salt and sand hanging in the air around us.

After a long silence, Davey suddenly spoke. "Come on, Finn. There's still an hour till low tide. No point waiting. The seagulls won't bother in the dark."

"You sure?" I asked. I didn't want to risk anything going wrong now.

"Yeah. Just make sure you're here before low tide in the morning."

We turned and walked back, just as the first of the rain began to fall. I felt elated, happy to be alive, out there in the middle of nowhere with Davey.

Back on the road, almost half a mile away, I noticed a light. It had to be Dad, back from sea unexpectedly and out looking for me. Words began to tumble through my mind, none of which would make any difference to him. I'd let Dad down, and there would be no reasoning with him. I prayed urgently for some luck, for it only to be Quigley.

As we got closer, Davey suddenly raised a hand to his mouth and whistled. A moment later, a similar whistle returned to us across the sand, almost lost in the wind.

"Dad," he explained as I looked across at him, and a surge of relief flew up through my chest and out with my next breath. When we arrived on the road I saw in the small ring of light a bucket half full of cockles on the ground next to Mr. Finer.

Mr. Finer held up the paraffin lamp.

"Hello Finn," he said. "Davey told me about the contest today." He smiled warmly, and I noticed him take Davey's

hand in his. Dad hadn't done that to me for a long time. "Well, we'd best be going. Good luck, now!" They turned and wandered slowly away in the direction of the land's end, the sky a vast black canopy above them, leaving me alone on the dark road back to Seamer Bay. For a minute or two I watched their light getting smaller and fainter. Then I picked my bike from the bushes and turned for home.

That night I struggled to sleep, listening to the howling wind whip the side of the house. If I strained my ears, I could hear the roar of the sea and the muffled sound of the bell on the lightship, somewhere out in the mouth of the river. In my mind's strange, fluid world, just before sleep finally drowns the day, I saw huge crashing waves in the darkness and shuddered underneath my blankets.

Before first light, I rose and dressed quickly in the cold bedroom, creeping out of the house without breakfast, praying I didn't see Dad walking up from the harbor. Several times over the last week I'd decided to tell him the truth, but then changed my mind at the last minute. I was certain that he'd stop me from going down on the point. And that was my one chance of winning the contest.

Out in the cold, early-morning darkness I noticed two of my friends and their dads riding out of the village in different directions, heads down against the wind, buckets and knives fastened to bikes or wheelbarrows. But neither of them went my way. There was no sign of Dad either.

Quigley was going to meet me on the road to Clee Point at eight.

"You don't have to come down on the beach with me, Quigley," I'd suggested. "You could just meet me later to check the line."

I was so relieved when he nodded. "No point really, I suppose. I helped you make it, didn't I?" he laughed. Now I could get the line from Davey's creek without anyone knowing. All I had to do was get back on the road before eight, and hope Quigley wasn't early.

The walk out to the creek was long and lonely. By the shore, godwits and redshank flew up in front of me, warning me away from their nests. As I approached the place where we'd set the line, I saw that I was too early. Only the tops of the stakes could be seen in the shallow water. I watched and waited, my heart pounding with anticipation. I even dared to imagine my name on the brass plate at the fish market later that day. But there was also a cautious voice arguing in my head, preparing me for failure. It sounded like Dad's voice.

Then I saw a thrashing in the water as the tide began to edge away and the fish were left stranded in the shallows.

I moved in closer. The sea around the line was now boiling with movement. I unhooked the first fish and tossed it into the bucket. Then the next, and the next... Every hook revealed the mottled back of a large codling.

Seventy-nine fish! It took three trips with the bucket to fill the covered wheelbarrow on the back of my bike. Each time, I prayed the gulls didn't carry any of them off while I was gone. When I'd finished, I pedaled back down the road into the wind, the rain stinging my face.

Quigley wasn't there when I reached our meeting place. I could just see a faint speck moving toward me along the road from Seamer Bay. I put my head back, looked up at the rain clouds scuttling past overhead and laughed out loud into the wind.

CHAPTER ELEVEN

A WINNER

M a was already dressed for church when I came in. "Hurry up, Finn! You're filthy. Go and wash quickly or we'll be late."

Dad sat quietly in his chair in the corner. He'd been out on the boat overnight and looked tired. As I passed him, he reached out, his hand resting on my arm for a moment before sliding off again.

"Quigley told me you've a chance."

I looked down at my woolen socks. "Suppose so. We all have. It's just luck."

"Nah. There's no luck in it." I waited for the next comment, but it never came. He studied me for a moment. "So?" I didn't understand what he meant. "Well? What did you get then?" he asked.

I stood there, smiling, wanting to tell him. "Come to the fish market later. You'll see."

The church was full by the time we arrived. Everyone I knew, except Dad and the Finers, was there. Even Quigley had sneaked in at the back and winked at me as I passed. Never in my life had an hour lasted so long. The children eyed each other suspiciously. The priest spoke at length from the pulpit, reminding everyone at the end about the contest after church.

"We shall see which of our children will win this wonderful prize." He held the blue-and-white boat up to the worshippers and there was a soft rumble of approval. Sitting near the front, old Joe McKinnon turned around and smiled with satisfaction at the stir he had caused among the villagers.

At last, the priest stood by the door at the back of the church and shook hands with people as they left. The adults stopped and chatted to each other, but the set-liners had already escaped home to collect their fish.

The fish market had always been my favorite place in the village — the rows and rows of kits brimming with fish, the shouts of the auctioneer and the buyers, the jokes of the fishermen, the smell of fish and salt — and early morning was always the best time, just after the boats had landed their catches. But the fish market had never been open on a Sunday, until today.

The large wooden shed on the quay was packed to the doors. I began to realize how nervous I felt, standing there behind my covered wheelbarrow in the line of children that had formed at the far end. Suddenly, there was a burst of activity in the crowd and Joe McKinnon broke through to the makeshift stage that had been built from old kits and boxes. In his hand was the blue-and-white model boat. He raised it in the air and the crowd suddenly fell silent.

"On behalf of the Fishermen's Committee, I welcome you all to the first annual village set-lining contest. The child with the most fish from a hundred-hook line set on last night's tide will win this wonderful boat for the year. Also they will have the honor of seeing their name displayed on the plate, and on our new board, as the first ever winner." He indicated a gleaming oak board inscribed

with gold letters at the back of the market shed. "Now!" He stared down at the twenty or so children who had lined up their wheelbarrows in front of him, and fixed a thin smile to his face. "Who has thirty?!"

Nobody moved, and Joe McKinnon looked over our heads to the crowd behind and smiled. There was laughter from the crowd, and some of the fishermen behind me whistled loudly.

Joe raised his hand for calm. "Good. Let's try a little higher, shall we? Who has fifty?"

I looked sideways, and saw the hope drain from many of the liners' faces. Most of the children sank back slowly into the crowd with their wheelbarrows. There were only four of us left. I turned and looked out over the crowd for Dad, but there was no sign of him.

"You have all done very well to beat fifty, but of course only one of you can win. So…let's see! Does anybody have sixty?" Joe asked.

Two of the boys groaned, turned and walked away from him. One other boy was left next to me. We looked at each other and grinned nervously. But we both knew that in a few seconds one of us would not be smiling. There was a low excited whispering from the crowd.

"Well done, boys. Well done! But only one of you can win, I'm afraid." He paused, drawing the moment out, teasing the crowd. Then he took a deep breath and spoke. "Step forward if you have seventy."

I stepped forward, eyes fixed on Joe McKinnon, not daring to look sideways. There seemed to be a moment where time froze under his blue eyes and the murmur of the crowd. Everything was still. Suddenly, there was a huge cheer; I looked to my right and saw an empty space. Then I was hoisted from behind into the air and onto someone's shoulders, with hands from the crowd trying to slap my back. All around were smiles directed at me, even from the defeated liners. When I looked down I saw familiar thick, wavy hair. It was Dad. I placed my hands on top of his head to steady myself and he reached up and clasped them in his, holding them out to the sides as he danced a jig of delight.

"My son, the champion set-liner!" From high above I could only imagine the smile on his face.

"Here, Quigley!" He changed course through the sea of bodies until he found what he was looking for. "Did you see, Quigley? Hasn't he done you proud?" Quigley smiled and nodded, knocking his pipe against the wall. Then he looked up at me.

"Grand, Finn. Grand!"

As we left the shed and headed down the quay toward the village, the boat clasped tightly in my hands and the crowd streaming out behind us, I looked back for a moment along the quay. There at the far end, away from the crowd, hands deep in his coat pockets and shoulders hunched against the cold, was Davey Finer, watching the procession.

91

During the afternoon, the weather worsened and the villagers closed their shutters for the night. For a few hours I had been famous. At dinner I was put at the head of the table and the boat placed in front of me for all to see. Later in the afternoon, many of the other liners came to call to swap stories and admire the boat. In spite of their persistent questions, I couldn't tell them where I'd set the line, not in front of Ma and Dad.

"I'm not telling you. It's my secret," I joked with them. Dad ruffled my hair and smiled.

It was after they'd gone that a feeling began to grow inside me. At first it was just an uneasiness, but I couldn't think what was causing it. By the end of the afternoon everything felt wrong. I sat with the boat on my lap, staring at the flames of the fire gusting in the draft down the chimney. I let my mind drift back over the day's events. It felt like such a long time since I rode out in the early morning and so much had happened. Finally, I recalled the image of Dad, Quigley and me leaving the market shed in the middle of the crowd.

As I thought of Davey, standing alone at the end of the quay, away from the excitement of the contest, I began to realize what was bothering me. The boat was not mine. Not just mine, anyway. It was Davey who had shown me the best ground. It was Davey who had shown me the shape of the line. It was Davey who had told me to cover the hooks with sand. He'd even helped me to set the line. He should at least have shared in the glory, and everyone should know about it.

I hadn't cheated. The rules had been followed. But I might never have won without Davey. Suddenly, I felt like I'd betrayed him, like I'd let him down somehow. There, in the fish market, I'd had a chance to get the other boys to accept him, to show them how good at fishing he was. But I'd let myself get caught up in the excitement of the contest and forgotten all about him. And next week, when I saw my name on the board in the fish market, I would know that really there should be another name next to mine—Davey Finer.

I looked down at the boat gleaming in the firelight and felt a surge of guilt. Dad was asleep in a chair in the corner. Ma was upstairs. Without thinking, I grabbed my coat and slipped quietly away out the back door into the chaos of the storm.

CHAPTER TWELVE

A STORMY NIGHT

It was already dark as I cycled down to Clee Point. On the east side I could hear huge waves crashing into the sand, but the image of Davey on the quayside and the shame that I felt helped to keep my mind off the danger I was putting myself in. It was hard to see the road as spray flew across my path. Twice I braked hard and waited, listening to the roaring of the waves, wondering whether to be sensible and turn back for home. I could always come down the next day, after all. Or Davey might even make it to school if the storm died down. But something drove me forward each time.

As I neared the end of the point, I suddenly had to brake hard. In front of me there was water rushing over the road from the sea to the river. There was no way across. I heard the faint sound of voices, urgent voices, in the blackness ahead. I stood confused for a moment, just as I'd been the

day I was nearly cut off by the tide on Fleet Sand, trying
to make sense of what was in front of me. Then I realized
what must have happened. There'd been a breach. In
front of me, somewhere out there in the dark night, the
thrashing waves had created an island. The voices belonged
to the Finers. And they were trapped.

"Davey!" I shouted into the wind. But it was useless.
Nobody could be heard on a night like this. For a minute
I stood, my legs apart, braced against the northwesterly
wind at my back. There seemed little I could do to help them.

Then, just as I was about to get back on my bike and
ride to the village to get help, I heard the voices again. From
the darkness, in the direction of where I imagined the house
to be, I saw something move. It was Mr. Finer, followed
closely by Kitty and Davey. Mr. Finer was carrying a coil
of rope over one shoulder. As they approached the breach,
where the waves were still crashing, Davey looked across
and noticed me. For a moment he just stared, as though he
couldn't believe what he was seeing. Then he tugged his
dad's sleeve and pointed at me.

"Finn!... Catch this!" Mr. Finer called against the wind,
and flung one end of the rope across the breach water. It
landed near my feet and I quickly grabbed it and held on
tight. I watched Mr. Finer lash his end to a stake which

he then hammered into the sand. "...ight, hold...Finn! Kitty's com...ross!" he cupped his hands and shouted into the wind.

There was little I could do but watch as Kitty held on to the rope and began to wade across the water. She sobbed with fright as she walked but she was brave, and soon she was halfway across.

"...eep hold...itty!" Mr. Finer shouted. "...be okay."

She didn't look back at him, concentrating on the rope and how deep the water was getting. Then suddenly, as it neared her waist, a huge wave came out of the darkness and crashed across the breach. I turned away from the wave just as it came down, but not before I heard Kitty shriek as she lost her balance.

A second or so later I turned back, expecting the worst. But she was still there, soaked, clinging to the rope and hauling herself toward me.

"Kitty!" I heard Mr. Finer shouting across the breach.

"She's okay! She's nearly there!" I cried. I held the rope fast with one hand, reached out with the other and grabbed her, pulling her away from the water. She fell to her knees, sobbing.

When I looked back across the breach, I saw Davey starting the same journey. He'd barely reached the middle

when I heard a rumble which sounded like thunder, followed by an enormous wave crashing across the point.

"Davey! Look out…" I screamed, but the wave hit me in the side and knocked me over. When I stood up again, I realized my hands were empty. The rope had gone. "Davey!" I shouted into the blackness. Across on the other side I saw Mr. Finer urgently hauling at the rope with all his strength.

"Finn!" he called into the wind, both hands cupped around his mouth. "…vey's here…okay…too danger… now…et help!"

I waved at him to let him know I'd understood. Kitty was still on her knees.

"Come on, Kitty." I pulled her up by the hands and helped her toward my bike. "You ever had a backy?" I smiled, climbing onto my bike. She wiped a hand across her face and tried a grin.

"What do you think?" she said, and pushed herself up onto the seat.

I pedaled hard but we were heading into the wind now, and there were two of us on the bike. Kitty held me tightly around the waist, and I could feel her wet head resting on my back. For the first time I felt like I was in charge, that she needed my help. Even in the time I'd been down there, the storm had gotten worse. My thigh muscles were

beginning to burn with the effort of standing up on the pedals, so I was relieved when the land started to widen and we saw the lights of the harbor entrance.

I turned the brass handle of The Anchor's door and we were thrown inside by the wind. Behind the door somebody cursed and kicked it shut. Dad saw me and stood up quickly.

"Finn! What is it? Where have you been?" There was no time for long explanations. Kitty stood slightly behind me, her face white and drawn, hair plastered to her skull from the sea and the rain.

"Dad! There's been a breach on Clee Point!" I panted. The men seated around the barroom looked on in silence.

"What? How do you…?" He stared at Kitty with sudden understanding. "Have you been down there, Finn? I warned you…" He walked toward me.

"Dad! There's been a breach! We have to do something!"

I looked around at the stern faces of the men. Some of them I knew well, men like Jack Screaton and Reuben Knaggs who worked in Dad's crew. They lived hard lives, I knew. And here was a boy in a man's place, demanding things of his father, daring to speak like an adult. It would make them cross, and Dad would have to show them his authority.

"There's nothing we can do, son. It was bound to happen." Dad looked embarrassed as he came close and whispered in my ear. "Now go home. You're soaked to the bone. Tell your ma I'll not be long."

I stared at him, then looked around at the cozy bar with its lamps and fire and pipe smoke. I knew Dad wanted me to turn and walk out the door. But I'd let Kitty and Davey down once, in the yard at school, and I wasn't going to do it again.

"You can't all just sit here — they'll drown! We helped Kitty across but then the waves became too strong and I lost the rope. You've got to help!" My voice was loud and I felt myself trembling.

"Now calm down, son. Come on, now. It's too dangerous." Dad put a hand on my shoulder.

One of the older men laughed. "Hey! What do you think that old hermit would do if it was us down there and him in here? Ask yourself that, lad!" There was a brief muttering of agreement in the room. I looked at Dad again. He seemed stuck, not knowing what to do, where to turn. My face flushed with anger. They didn't seem to care that Kitty was standing in the room with us. Then Joe McKinnon stood up. I hadn't noticed him sitting at a table near the door.

"Come on now, Finn. We've talked about this before, haven't we?"

Dad turned to him, confused. Joe looked at Kitty but she wouldn't catch his eye. Her eyes were fixed on the flames of the fire. The night's events seemed to have left her in a state of shock.

I looked at the men sitting at tables, and my anger welled up through my chest. "You're all hard men," I said. "The sea has made you hard. But you're hard inside too! He has Davey down there with him. They've never hurt anyone. And Mr. Finer, I know what you all say about him. And it's all lies, because he's a good man. I've spoken to him, which is more than any of you have ever tried to do. And he's always kind to me. He never let his mates down on that boat…and he loved his wife. He just wanted to be near her…" I glanced toward Joe McKinnon. "…and you want to blame him just because…" I didn't finish the sentence. I knew I'd gone too far. Joe glared back at me, but I was determined to say what was on my mind. "I'm not surprised he hardly ever comes to the village, if that's how he's treated."

I suddenly became conscious of my own voice echoing off the walls. The room soon filled with silence, except for the violence of the storm outside. Kitty was still staring at the flames.

"We can't leave them. They'll lose everything they've got. I've got to go back and…" I began, but Dad interrupted me. He'd been watching me speak, a distant look in his eyes, his forehead slowly wrinkling.

"No, you're not, Finn." He held my arm fast as I tried to turn for the door. "It's too dangerous. You're staying here, where it's safe." He stared down at his shoes. "I'll go." He turned to the men at the tables and looked at them straight. "He's right. We can't leave them in danger down there without trying to help."

There was a murmur of disapproval from the men. Joe McKinnon walked over to Dad.

"Come on now, Tom. There's no point in risking our lives for..." He glanced over at Kitty, who was still standing behind me, by the door, afraid to come any further in. Joe turned his back to her, and whispered something to Dad.

Dad stared at him for a long time, then slowly his head began to shake from side to side.

"What kind of man are you, Joe? You'd leave a man and his lad to drown, would you? Chairman of the Fishermen's Committee? We're supposed to help each other!" he said.

"You know what he did! If it wasn't for him..." Joe began.

"No, Joe. You don't know that. We don't know that. Nobody knows what happened that night, except Bill Finer. But you've never asked him, have you? You've invented your own story, Joe." There was a long pause. Joe looked shocked to hear Dad speak to him like this. Most of the other men stared hard at their boots. "I know this much, though," Dad continued after a while. "Bill Finer's son saved Finn from drowning. So I have to try and help. I owe him that, at least." He addressed the men at the tables. "Is anybody coming? If not, I'll go on my own."

There was a long silence. Only the crackling of the logs on the fire and the wind in the casements could be heard. Then suddenly, from a dark corner of the room, there was a rustling of oilskins and somebody stood, walking slowly forward out of the shadows. It was Quigley. Dad saw him and smiled.

"Quigley. Good man." Then, one by one, the men began to stand and follow Dad out into the storm until only Joe McKinnon was left.

CHAPTER THIRTEEN

RESCUE IN THE NIGHT

Dad had quickly organized the men and they'd taken rope, life preservers and a small rowing boat that they'd managed to haul up onto a cart. I watched them begin the long walk down to Clee Point, straining to pull the cart, two men on each side to keep the boat steady on top. They were soon lost in the night.

Ma came in to persuade me and Kitty to go home with her, but I wouldn't move from the inn. She didn't argue. Instead she brought us blankets and some dry clothes. Ma helped Kitty change, telling her everything would be all right. I wasn't so sure.

I peered out into the moonless dark. Everywhere was black but you could hear the wind howling, the waves crashing violently against the harbor wall and a lashing sound as the spray reared up and over onto the quayside. There was nobody out there on a night like this. Nobody, that is, except the men who'd followed Dad and Quigley down the road to the point.

"Don't worry, Finn. They'll find them." Ma rubbed my back gently.

I sat by the window most of the night while Kitty tossed and turned on one of the benches. The clock on the wall ticked off an hour, then two. I must have fallen asleep on the bench at some point because I was woken by the distant sound of a cart and men's voices. Looking out of the window again, I saw some lights bobbing in the darkness. At first I thought they must be from boats out at sea, seeking the shelter of the harbor, but soon I realized it was the men walking back by the seawall from the road.

Twenty minutes later, the door flew open and in a confusion of shouting, wind, bodies and wet clothes I saw Mr. Finer carry Davey in his arms and lay him on a bench. He wasn't moving. Kitty, her eyes red from lack of sleep, jumped up and ran across the room when she saw them. One of the men built up the fire again. Last of all came Dad with Quigley, carrying some boxes and a few bags. They put them down in the corner where Mr. Finer now sat, stroking his son's hair. Davey was motionless. There was a dread hush in the room as the men sat down in silence, watching.

"Finn. Time for bed, now. There's nothing to be done 'til morning. Dr. Ackland's on his way." Dad took my hand and led me out into the wild night.

At home I slept fitfully, waking and remembering the night's events, then drifting back to sleep for a while. There were times when I could hear whispered voices downstairs. At one point I woke and was sure I could smell cooking.

Finally, as the first gray light of dawn appeared through the shutters, I got up, unable to sleep any longer. Outside on the landing, I bumped into Ma coming out of the spare room. She put her fingers to her lips.

"You all right, Finn?" she said.

I nodded. "Why you being quiet?" I asked.

She looked at the closed door of the bedroom. "We brought him here so he could have a bed," she whispered. Her brow wrinkled, in the way it always did when she was worried. "He got very cold. Dr. Ackland says to warm him slowly, but he's not woken yet."

"Can I go in?" I asked. I wanted to be there, to help Davey.

"No. His dad's in with him. Give them time."

Ma took me downstairs to the kitchen where she'd built a big fire. Kitty was curled up asleep on the big chair where Dad usually sat with his newspaper. Someone had put a blanket over her.

"Here, have some soup," Ma said, fetching a bowl out of the cupboard. That must have been what I could smell when I woke in the night. As I ate some soup, soaking it up with chunks of Ma's bread, the kitchen door opened and the cold, clear air rushed in.

"Mmm. Smells good," Dad said, taking a piece of the bread and dipping it in my soup. He took off his oilskin jacket and sat down at the table and unlaced his boots. "At least the storm's blown itself out." Ma suddenly noticed the boots.

"Will you look at the state of them! Come on — out!" she whispered, mindful of Kitty still asleep on the chair, and shooed him back out the door.

"Me and Quigley went back down the point at first light to see the damage. He's stayed to see what he can salvage," Dad said, coming back through the door in his socks.

"What's it like?" Ma whispered, looking over at Kitty.

Dad shook his head sadly. "It's a wreck. They can't go back, not for weeks at least. They'll have to stay here."

"Can I go down there and help Quigley?" I said.

Dad looked at me and smiled. "No, Finn. Best not. He'll be fine on his own."

"What about Davey?" I asked. Dad and Ma exchanged a glance and I knew I wasn't going to get a real answer.

"We just have to wait and see, Finn. You get ready for school. It'll take your mind off things," Ma said, taking my empty bowl away.

At school everyone wanted to hear about the contest. They asked me questions, trying to find out where I'd set the line, but it didn't feel so important now and I had little to say. On the day I should have been the talk of the school, they soon lost interest in me.

All morning I stared out the window at the clear sky over the sea, thinking about the day before. As usual, nobody had even noticed that Davey and Kitty were absent. Some people had heard about the breach, but they showed no concern for the Finers.

At lunchtime I stood alone in the yard as my friends played football. They seemed like strangers to me now. All I could think about was the damage the sea had done to the Finers' lives. Then it struck me that it wasn't just the sea to blame. It was us, the villagers. If we'd been kinder to them, they may never have stayed down there on Clee Point.

I came to a decision. I sneaked out of the school yard by the side gate and ran home. Hiding behind the coal shed in the back garden, I took my bike from against the wall as soon as I saw Ma go out, and then pedaled hard down the long road to Clee Point. I was going to help. I was sure

Quigley would welcome an extra pair of hands, in spite of what Dad had said.

I shot straight through the breach water with my legs in the air, now it had receded a little. Nearing the end of the point, I spotted someone dragging something out of the house; a table, it looked like. As the figure emerged into the sunlight I saw it was Quigley. Then I became aware of another man holding on to the other end. It was Dad.

I smiled to myself, and rode quickly back to school before lunchtime was over.

Pushing my bike on the way home from school that afternoon I saw Kitty, walking up the hill with a bag full of vegetables from the market.

"Just getting these for your ma," she said, smiling at me.

"How's Davey?" I asked, as we began to walk back to the house.

She looked up at the sky. "Dad's been with him all day. He won't say. I think he's frightened…" She stopped and turned to me. There was something in her eyes, a tear perhaps, or just a reflection of the light from the low sun. I wanted to make her feel better, but I didn't know how. She watched me calmly and I desperately wanted to speak, to say something grown up to her. But I couldn't find the words.

"Thank you, Finn," she said.

I was puzzled. "What for?" I asked.

"Well, for speaking your mind. You're not so bad after all!"

She laughed suddenly and turned. I watched her as she walked off ahead of me, her tangled black hair like frayed rope ends.

CHAPTER FOURTEEN

AN END AND A BEGINNING

For the next two days, the faces in our house were serious and thoughtful. I saw very little of Mr. Finer. He'd come into the kitchen occasionally and talk in whispers to Ma or Dad. He always left a smile for me as he went back up the stairs, but I found out very little about Davey. I knew though from their faces that he was very ill. Kitty stayed with us in the kitchen most of the time, reading or helping Ma out. She was only a year older than me, but she could do everything Ma did. Ma had made her a bed on the front-room floor from cushions and blankets.

"Maggie! He's awake!" Kitty said, rushing downstairs on the second evening. I saw relief flood through Ma's face. Dad was talking to Quigley in the backyard. "Hey, you two!" she shouted, opening the door. "Davey's awake!"

They came in quickly.

"Hey, now that's great news," Dad said.

Kitty smiled at him. "He's still weak, but I think he'll be all right."

"I'll take him some sweet tea. It'll help get his strength up," Ma said.

"What's up, there, Finn?" Dad said to me.

It was only then that I felt the tears streaming down my cheeks — tears of relief. I rubbed my eyes quickly on my sleeve. "Nothing," I said, but I knew Kitty was watching me.

The next day I was allowed up to see Davey on my own. I took the blue and white boat up with me.

"Not too long, eh, Finn? He still needs a lot of rest," Mr. Finer said, standing outside the bedroom. He'd slept for three nights in a chair by the bed and he looked exhausted.

Davey was propped up on some pillows and the room was warmed by a small fire in the grate. It was the first time I'd ever seen a fire in there. He smiled at me as I sat down in the chair.

"You okay?" I asked.

"Yeah. A bit better now, thanks. Dad said I owe my life to you and your dad," he said. I looked at the floor. "Anyway, what were you doing down on the point at night?"

"Coming to see you," I replied, looking up again.

"Why?"

"Well, I...I wanted to say something."

Davey looked puzzled, and shifted his weight a little to turn his body toward me. "What?" he asked.

"The contest. You helped me win it. I thought we should share the boat. Get both our names on the board at the fish market. That's all," I said.

Davey looked thoughtfully at the boat in my lap. "I don't think the committee would like that, Finn. They wouldn't want a Finer to win. It's against the rules, too. It has to be just one person. And it was your line, not mine." He smiled. "I'm not bothered about a stupid boat anyway."

There was a pause as he caught my eye, then we both burst out laughing.

Two days later they left our house, and Seamer Bay. Kitty and Davey walked behind their father, who pushed a large wooden cart full of the belongings he and Dad and Quigley had managed to save. Their boat had been washed away and the ground floor of the house flooded, and although the sea had retreated, it would not be long before it came back to stay. The very end of the point would soon become an island. They couldn't live there anymore.

Kitty and Davey stood by the cart outside our house and I ran out to see them.

"You could visit us," Davey said, raising his eyes to mine and smiling sadly.

"If you want to, that is?" Kitty flashed a grin at me and leaned on the side of the cart. I was going to miss them, all of them.

"Definitely. I will." I saw Kitty watching me, as she always did. It was like she forced the truth from me with that look. "Promise!" I laughed.

I saw Ma and Dad and Mr. Finer talking by the front door. Then I saw him take a brown-paper package from inside his coat and give it to Dad, and they all shook hands. Then Mr. Finer walked slowly over to us by the cart.

"You ready?" he said. Kitty and Davey lifted their heads and nodded. Mr. Finer looked at me and put out his hand to shake mine. His grasp was firm. "Good luck, Finn. And thank you. Keep going with the lines. Davey told me you won!" I nodded. He smiled and picked up the handles of the cart. "Good-bye, Finn."

Dad looked thoughtful, almost sad, as they began to walk away up the hill.

"Why're they going?" I asked, as we watched them leave.

"Mr. Finer wants to start again. He's lost his house, his boat and his living."

"Where will they go?"

"I found him a job up the coast in Burnsea on a long-lining crew. And a small cottage to rent," Dad replied.

"But couldn't they stay?" I asked.

Dad shrugged his shoulders and put his arm around me. "I tried to change his mind. Offered to help him build a new house nearer the village. But he didn't want to stay. I can't say I blame him."

Dad looked up the hill as the Finers drew further away from us. There wasn't a cloud in the sky. Ma put her arms around me from behind and squeezed me, resting her chin on my shoulder. I could feel the warmth of her breath on my ear.

"They'll only be four miles away, Finn. You could cycle up there on the weekends if you wanted? And they'll be back to visit their ma's grave, won't they? She'll have a whole island to herself soon."

It didn't seem fair. They were the ones going away, leaving their mother behind, and it wasn't their fault. Tears started to roll down my cheeks. Ma pulled me to her and I buried my face in her shawl.

"There, Finn. You can't stop the sea, can you? They'll be all right. Their dad'll see to that," she whispered into my hair.

The few people they passed on their way out of the village looked down at the road, but the Finers held their heads forward. As they drew almost out of sight, I saw Davey turn and look back. I waved, but I wasn't sure if he saw.

"Finn?" I looked behind me. Ma had gone back inside the house but Dad was still standing in the middle of the road watching them go. "Mr. Finer wanted you to have this." He passed me the brown-paper package. I sat down on the front step of our house and undid the string. Inside was a small carved wooden chess set in a fold-up box, the same set I'd played with at their house. Dad wandered over and touched my shoulder lightly. "He said you know how to play?" I nodded, fighting the tears at the back of my throat. Dad picked up a black pawn from the open box and turned it over in his hands. "Well, Quigley don't like games much, so I supposed you'd better teach me."

I carried on setting lines that winter, sometimes with Quigley, sometimes on my own. When Dad came in, he always wanted to know how many I'd caught.

"How do you do it, lad? I don't remember getting as many when I was your age." He watched Ma filleting the fish with a long-handled knife at the kitchen table. Every evening we'd finish supper and then he'd fetch the chess set to the table, reading his newspaper in between moves. "You're making plenty of money, I suppose?" he laughed.

He was right. Quigley was selling the fish at market for me and I was saving up fast. And when I had enough I was going to buy a model boat, and ride my bike four miles up the coast to Burnsea.

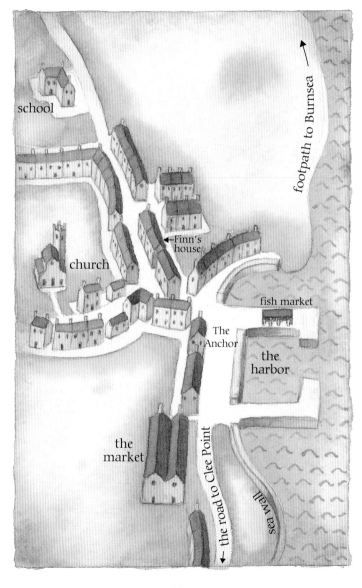

school

footpath to Burnsea →

←Finn's house

church

fish market

The Anchor

the harbor

the market

the road to Clee Point

sea wall

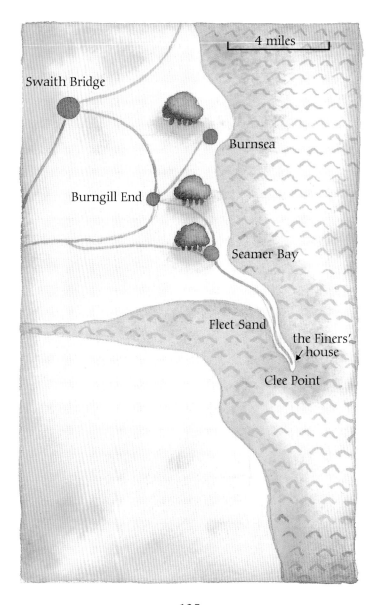

Swaith Bridge

Burnsea

Burngill End

Seamer Bay

Fleet Sand

the Finers' house

Clee Point

4 miles

Glossary

boom the spa, or long pole, that is attached to the mast of a sailing boat and to which the mainsail is fastened

bow the front end of a boat

breach the place where the sea breaks through the spit

buckthorn *see* sea buckthorn

cobblestones large stones packed together to make a road or path

coble a small, open fishing boat

cockles small edible shellfish found in the sand

codling a young cod

conger eel a long, snake-like, slippery fish

creek a small river running out across the sand to the sea

cuddy a small open cabin in the bow of a boat

curlew a wading bird with a long, curved bill

dab a flat fish found in an estuary

estuary the mouth of a river where it joins the sea; the water there is seawater

filleting removing the bones, head and tail of a fish to make it ready to cook and eat

flounder a flat fish found in an estuary

godwit a wading bird like a curlew

gunwale the upper edge of the side of a boat

half-blood knot a type of knot used by fishermen to attach a fishing line to a hook

herring a small, silvery fish caught off the coast in nets

hull the body of a boat

jetty a long platform sticking out into the sea where a boat can be tied up

kit a big tub, box or basket for holding fish after they have been caught

kit bag a large, cloth bag used by fishermen to carry their belongings

lightship a small ship, anchored at sea, with a light attached to show the way

lobster a large, edible shellfish with claws

long-lining a way of fishing from a boat using a long line held down by anchors and to which many hooks are attached

lugworm a large worm found in sand and used by fishermen as bait for fish

mainsail the largest sail on a boat, attached along one edge to the mast and along the bottom edge to the boom

marram grass thin, reedy grass that grows in sand

oilskins clothes made from cloth waterproofed with oil

oystercatcher a wading sea bird with a long beak for prying open shellfish

quay a landing place at a harbor

redshank a wading sea bird with long red legs

samphire a plant with fleshy leaves that you can eat, found on or near the seashore

sea-buckthorn a thorny bush with orange berries that grows well in sandy ground

set-lining fishing using a line fastened to stakes or posts pushed into the sand at low tide and with baited hooks attached to it; when the tide comes in, fish eat the bait and get caught

snipe a wading sea bird found on flat, marshy land

spit a long, thin stretch of land sticking out into the sea

stake a piece of wood, sharpened at one end for pushing into the earth or sand

stern the back end of a boat

tacking sailing by heading toward the wind in a zigzag pattern, often changing course, or "tack"

tiller short pole attached to the back of a boat and used for steering

twine strong thread made by twisting several strands together

whiting a small white fish found in an estuary